HANGED BY THE NECK

Caroline England

Copyright © 2019 Caroline England
All rights reserved.
ISBN-13: 978-10-9925767-4

To Belinda, with love

CONTENTS

Chosen	1
Al Fresco	15
Little Piece of Cheer	24
A Trouble Shared	29
The Delivery	38
Gone in an Instant	45
Wasted Time	51
A Reminder of Sin	61
Godliness	69
The Price of Silence	74
Time for Sleep	81
A Good Clean	86
About the Author	91
Also by Caroline England	92

CHOSEN

My first clear memory of Vanessa was in my last year of primary school. She wasn't my real aunt, but we called her Aunty on the rare occasions she visited us, despite her protestations.

'God, don't call me that. It makes me sound old. Nearly as old as your mum.'

My brother raised his head from the glossy magazine she had brought. 'But you *are* as old as Mum,' he said. 'You were in the same class at school.'

Mum turned from the sink and smiled. 'Thank you, Tim. That's why I have a son, Vanessa. They love their darling mothers.'

Mum ruffled Tim's hair, but her hand was wet with suds, so he didn't look pleased. I carried on with my sketch of the kettle.

'I see I'll have to bribe you to keep schtum, Timmy darling.' Vanessa tapped the magazine article with a knife. '*This* says I'm thirty-three, and so I must be. In fact, I like thirty-three; I think I'll stick with it.'

Her green eyes narrowing, Vanessa leaned over to peer at my drawing. Her hair was the colour of burned sunset. I had to resist the urge to touch it, to wrap it in my hands and bring it to my face.

'What are you drawing this time, sweetie? A chrome kettle! You don't make it easy on yourself. But you're good, very good!'

Ash fell from her cigarette and she brushed it off the parchment with long tapering fingers. Her nails, I noticed, were bitten to the quick. 'Oh, Lord, I've smudged it in. Sorry, sweetie.' She laughed with neat gleaming teeth. 'Maybe it helps with the shading?'

My heart thrashing, I nodded, inordinately pleased that a fragment of Vanessa was forever ingrained on the page.

'How was *don't you know who I am*?' Dad asked when he arrived home.

'Well, you know Vanessa...' Mum started.

'Mutton dressed as lamb,' Tim replied for her.

Mum frowned and tutted. 'Not nice, Timothy. I'm only forty-two, not quite mutton yet...'

'Well, I think she's amazing,' I added.

But nobody was listening.

I was a dumpy ten year old then; a plain girl who didn't feel much loved. Things hadn't improved by the time I was fourteen.

'Vanessa telephoned with news today. In June

she's marrying a toy-boy a good ten years younger,' Mum said to Dad at tea time. 'I suppose I shouldn't be surprised.'

'What does this toy-boy do?'

'He's an artist called Sergio,' Tim answered for her. 'He's actually very well thought of.'

'Gosh, he must be special to be chosen by Vanessa,' I commented.

But nobody was listening.

Mum had forgotten to mention the main reason for my aunty's call. 'Oh, by the way, Vanessa has asked if you'd like to be a bridesmaid,' she said later. 'Don't feel you have to say yes. I'm sure she's just being kind.'

Of course it was yes. I'd been *chosen*.

Over the next few weeks, the excitement was unbearable.

Mum studied me with a cocked head as June approached. 'A perm's the thing,' she advised. 'To soften your face.'

The dress rehearsal came around soon after. 'You don't have to do it if you don't want, sweetie,' Vanessa said, eyeing my hair. 'But I think you look beautiful. Don't you, Ruth?'

Mum didn't reply. She didn't have to; her expression said it all. And so did the mirror. The silk dress clung to my belly and I couldn't bear to even peek at the mass of tight curls.

I had never felt so ugly, but that didn't matter. I had still been chosen.

❖ ❖ ❖

I once asked Mum why she and Vanessa weren't *really* friends. Mum looked shocked. 'But of course we're friends! We're the best of friends. You do say some silly things at times. Go and tidy your room.'

My room was already tidy, and anyway, I thought I had worked it all out.

❖ ❖ ❖

I don't suppose my mother noticed when I packed my bags and left for university; she was still grieving for the loss of her perfect son to Fergus, a body builder from Rotherham.

I'd been offered a place at Goldsmiths' College to read music; my teachers were thrilled for me and so was Vanessa. A post card soon arrived from Venice:

'It's fate, honey. London bound! I'm not always at home but now we can get to know each other properly. Arrivederci!'

Though flattered, I tried to temper my excitement with a dose of (Mum-like) salt. Vanessa had become quite famous, had no need to say *'don't you know who I am'* anymore. But she didn't disappoint me; she swept through my halls of residence duly fancy and furred on the third Sunday of October, looking for me.

◆ ◆ ◆

When Vanessa wasn't away filming, Sundays were spent in Belgravia.

'You don't mind if we stay in?' she would ask, wearing one of her exquisite pairs of silk pyjamas. Her face, bare of make up, was more radiant than I had imagined. She still looked incredibly young and line-free.

'I'm so exhausted!' she'd continue. 'I need to lie down for a long time. Bernard will look after us, won't you, my love?'

I don't suppose anyone would have believed I spent the sabbath in a golden domed room, lounging on an emperor-sized bed with my every whim catered for by an elderly butler called Bernard. But then there was no one to tell. I didn't need friends; I had Vanessa.

◆ ◆ ◆

'What the fuck are you doing here?' a voice demanded from the landing.

I was taken by surprise - it was Sunday; I had rung the bell and Bernard had let me in as usual.

My heart thrashing, I looked up to Vanessa's husband. I hadn't seen Sergio since the wedding, but I barely recognised him; the black and sleek hair was no more - he'd shaved his head.

'She's not here,' he continued as he jerked towards the stairs. 'She should have told you...'

Wearing underpants and a white t-shirt smeared with oils, his face was a jigsaw of shadows. 'Get out. I can't stand kids. She knows that.'

Scrambling from the hallway to freedom, I pelted down the muffled streets, only stopping, eventually, to wipe tears from my burning cheeks. I hadn't felt that wounded or humiliated for a long time. I was angry too. Vanessa had betrayed me somehow, but it wasn't just that. I had cared too much; I was a fool.

I made a rare phone call to Mum that night.

'So, she's let you down already,' she stated, before I'd said a word.

Three Sundays later, Bernard arrived without warning to collect me in Vanessa's Rolls Royce. I was so relieved and pleased that the sour disappointment I had felt so keenly melted away and was forgotten.

Vanessa was animated; her auburn hair was shiny, her cheeks pink and lips red. Despite the heat, she was wearing a brightly coloured long kaftan.

'Shopping!' she declared when I arrived. 'We must have retail therapy today. Let's buy you clothes and shoes...and fur, even if it's faux!'

I looked down at my baggy t-shirt and combat trousers. 'Maybe give the fur a miss,' I replied, laughing.

I was chauffeured to Belgravia by Bernard after that. Nothing was mentioned about the missing weeks and a text would arrive from him to inform me if Vanessa was away. And occasionally a postcard would arrive:

'*Eiffel Tower, Honey! How quaint. Beaucoup d'amour. Vanessa.*'

Punctuated by shopping trips, the hairdressers and occasionally an art gallery '*to keep us cultured*', more lazy Sundays with Vanessa passed. She continued to buy me excessive amounts of expensive shoes and clothes, fragrance and make-up, but by then I had taken to them, enjoying the glow of her approval when I next arrived at her home.

Mum became ill; hospitalised with shingles, which was unusual, they said. Tim and Fergus were already there, but she seemed pleased to see me, surprisingly so.

'You must come home more often, love,' she said, clutching my hand. 'Your father and I really miss you.'

I nodded, distracted by a surge of emotion I couldn't quite identify. 'What beautiful flowers,' I said, focusing on a glorious bouquet of exotic plants.

I didn't need to read the card to see who they were from.

'She's not here, but you'll do.'

Sergio was sitting at the bottom of the stairs. He appeared different again. His hair had grown a little and he looked less gaunt, but his face was still dark and moody. I turned to search for Bernard, who'd said nothing of Vanessa's absence, but he'd gone, the door closed behind him.

Sergio stood and took my wrist. 'This way,' he stated, leading me to the back of the house.

We climbed dark rickety steps to the attic. Once at the top, light poured in through a roof window. Then a wall of heat hit me - it was stiflingly hot.

I finally exhaled. Like a naughty kid caught in grown up clothes, I stood open-mouthed and gaped at walls adorned by canvas after canvas. The poses and backgrounds were varied, but each one was of Vanessa, naked.

Sergio's voice pierced my building terror. 'Sit down,' he snapped. He pulled the ribbon from my hair and rearranged it around my cheeks and my shoulders. 'Relax. I only want your face today. You can strip the next time.'

I didn't see Vanessa again for a long time. Bernard still collected me on a Sunday and I posed for Sergio, sometimes naked, sometimes not. The conversation was limited to one word commands as he examined every contour of my face, or my arms, my breasts or my feet, with dark empty eyes. He'd sketch in charcoal or pencil on canvas, then sigh and disappear, sometimes for hours.

I sat and smoked and waited. Bernard continued his attempts to accommodate my every whim, but I didn't really care - nothing was the same without Vanessa.

Mum was hospitalised again; pneumonia this time, her immune system weakened by scarlett fever as a child. But this time there was no magnificent bouquet of flowers, or even a card. And that was when my feelings for my aunty began to change.

'Hey, everything OK?'

Sergio seemed anxious, attentive even. I'd skipped several weekends and whilst I didn't care about him, I felt vaguely guilty at the thought of Bernard sitting patiently in the Rolls outside my hall each missing Sunday.

His features smooth and boyish, Sergio tried

for a smile. 'You look nice. Beautiful. I've been waiting for you. We can eat first if you like...'

But I could see his foot tapping the stairs.

'No, that's fine,' I said, and I held out my hand.

The sittings seemed to progress after that. The commands receded as Sergio's face cleared. 'Perfetto!' he declared from time to time, before lapsing into silence. But at least he was painting.

From then on I remained in Belgravia. I slept in Vanessa's golden bedroom, wore her silk nightwear, and was coaxed into eating delicacies by Bernard. Vanessa wasn't mentioned by him or Sergio and I didn't ask. I tried to reason that I shouldn't take her absence so personally - if she had abandoned me, she'd done the same to her husband. But that made no difference; Vanessa had stolen my ten year old heart and she'd tossed it aside. That was unforgivable. And so when Sergio said, 'I need to have you right now,' I didn't say no.

I didn't tell Mum or Dad that I'd given up my course and my music, but I made the effort to see them more.

'You really are too thin,' Mum complained. 'I liked your hair short.'

'Who would have thought you'd grow into

Hanged by the Neck

such a beauty,' Dad declared.

'Watching out Tim, your sister's a bit of a stunner,' Fergus said.

'How on earth do you afford these lovely clothes?' Mum asked, touching the fur. 'And why do you wear such heavy make up? It makes you look far older than you are.'

But I wasn't offended. In some strange way, they admired me now.

'She wants to see you,' Sergio stated at breakfast one day.

'Who?'

'She's wanted to see you for a while,' he added, raking his hair.

Things had changed, but stayed the same. And Sergio had finished the first painting.

He couldn't make eye contact. 'I should have told you before, but...'

Though a man of few words, Bernard cleared his throat and revealed the truth in the car: Vanessa was ill; she had managed it for a long time, but the lucid periods were increasingly rare.

'I'm her father,' he said simply. 'It has been very difficult for us all. I'm glad you've been there.'

I thought of how this man had brought me

breakfast in Sergio's bed and I was swamped with guilt.

We lapsed into silence for the rest of the long journey, but Bernard eventually said 'we're here' and turned up a drive lined by huge glossy trees. A spectacular mansion finally greeted us at the top. It was almost a hotel, but with doors that were locked from the outside.

Almost breathless, I followed him to Vanessa's room, where he left me. A small replica of the bedroom in Belgravia, it took several seconds to drag my eyes from the golden walls and force them look at the bed. Filled with remorse and dread, I wondered if my aunty knew that I had betrayed her in the worst possible way.

Popped up against the pillows, Vanessa had tucked her feet to one side. Her face was so impassive, I was unable to read it. Was she in pain? What was she thinking? How did she feel? But one thing was for sure - she no longer resembled the woman I knew. Hair hidden by a turban, her face was tiny and pale, the skin stuck to her cheekbones. And she looked so very old.

'Oh, come on my darling girl, give me a smile,' she said, and for a moment I glimpsed the Vanessa I had adored.

She patted the cushion. 'Come and sit next to me. I want to look at you.'

I perched on the bed, my arms goose-bumped and body shaking, not only with remorse, but with fear.

She held out scrawny arms. 'Come on, sweetie, don't be shy. Lie down next to me. We used to do this, didn't we? Wasn't it fun?'

I nodded, my heart beating furiously, my mind in spasm. What could I possibly say to excuse what I'd done? Nothing. Nothing!

Vanessa leaned towards me. Her breath on my cheeks, she studied my face, then she traced its outline with her dry finger. My jaw, my chin; my eyebrows, my nose and my lips. It was all I could do to exhale. 'I always said you were beautiful, didn't I sweetie?'

Abruptly pulling away, she laughed, a small child's peal of delight, then she clapped her hands. 'Sergio thinks that he's the artist, but what a fine job I have done!'

'Sorry?' I managed to splutter through my alarm. Vanessa was still chortling and clapping wildly. My terror increased. What should I do? Call for help? Was there a bell I could ring?

Abruptly stopping the applause, she looked amused. 'Come and look!'

Climbing from the bed, she pulled me to the gilt mirror with surprising force. Then she removed her turban with a flourish. Patterned with a map of scores and scratches, her scalp was naked. Her eyes, I noticed, were grey.

She must have seen the look of mystification on my face. 'One moment, sweetie. The finishing touch!' she said, opening a drawer in the dresser.

She squashed the auburn wig on her head.

'There! Look! Who do you see?'

Almost paralysed, I stared at our reflections. I suppose I should have realised the day Sergio took down a painting of Vanessa and replaced it with me. I hadn't noticed the change for days.

Her eyes lit, Vanessa was still speaking. 'Look, sweetie, look at yourself. I painted you perfect and now you're me!'

She took my hand then. Mine was trembling; hers was papery firm. 'It isn't so bad is it, sweetie? He's a good lover, isn't he? The best I ever had! And there's Daddy too; they need you there and there you'll stay...'

My voice finally emerged, barely a whisper. 'And what about you?' I asked.

'Don't worry about me, sweetie. My work is complete!' She stroked my cheek softly and smiled, but her laugh was off key. 'Don't you see, my love? I've got what I wanted: now, I'll always be thirty-three!'

AL FRESCO

It was the road traffic signs that late April day. The constant reference to speed limits when Zita was the one flipping driving. That's when it started.

'It goes down to thirty soon. In anticipation of the village. You aren't slowing down. Are you listening, Zita?'

Not just the speedometer, driveshaft or damned torsion spring. Hump back bridges, level crossings, bus lanes and badgers. Changing gear too soon or too late. *Riding* the clutch; putting *strain* on the engine.

Strain, indeed! It was all just too much, especially when Zita had something to say. Couldn't Nigel *listen* for once? Pay attention and not interrupt? Take heed for a whole minute without a vindictive little swipe, or knowing *so* much better?

Putting life and limb in danger, she even broached it in the twenty mph zone: 'Please will you just listen to the story, Nigel, without passing comment?'

He glanced across with that 'what me?' look of hurt in his baby blue eyes. Then he graciously wafted his hand towards her, his mouth zipped almost for seconds, before: 'I think you'll find—'

Hitting the breaks hard, she brought the car to a shuddery stop. Snapping her head to the passenger seat, she actually raised her voice. And said several swear words. Only in retrospect did she analyse her astonishing reaction. Nigel had done exactly what she'd expected him to do. He'd interrupted her story after only moments, despite her preamble.

It was the predictability of it all. Like an old married couple.

Nigel was married, but not to Zita. Zita had expected him to wed her, had longed for the day they'd live together in happy concert as man and wife. They'd dated since university and she assumed they still were when Nigel rucked up on a Wednesday evening (for the usual *shaking of the sheets*) only (later) to learn he was getting hitched. Not just to someone, but to her old schoolfriend, Lucinda.

Luscious Lucinda with the double D lips and child bearing hips.

That seemed predictable too.

Zita missed Nigel's handsome face, if not his constant reminders that she was 'in debt' for climaxing when he didn't. 'Don't forget you're in debt. You owe me one,' he used to say. By phone, in person and by text.

That had been the trouble with Nigel. It hadn't always happened, but when it had, it was spectacular. And hard not to keep her raptures muted. 'Too noisy, Zita. It puts me off my stride,' he'd tut, rolling aside. Hence the occasional arrears, which she'd repaid *al fresco*. Just to please Nigel.

But, of course, Nigel had married someone else. It was hard for Zita to watch him and Lucinda in gurning wedded bliss. Even harder to feign a smile when baby Lucindas were regularly pelleted out. Yet slowly she became accustomed to Wednesdays alone. She eventually met one or two nice chaps who didn't criticise what she wore, the way she walked, applied her lipstick or talked, who admired her soft hair and fine eyes, even if they never quite succeeded in taking her to the heights of that exquisite *petite mort*.

After five bumpy years, Zita had become used to life *sans* Nigel. It wasn't all bad - she had her job at the library and there was the pleasure of wearing fashionable clothes and delicate shoes without having to worry about an impromptu request to kneel on a damp hillock or mound of leaves. She could *ride* the clutch and *strain* the engine at pleasure. There were no debts to be paid, no reminders to pay them by phone, in person or by text.

But Nigel came back.

Perhaps Lucinda didn't appreciate the great outdoors; maybe she didn't take an interest in torsion strings. It was even possible that Nigel had missed Zita. And this time it was different. No longer did he appear on a Wednesday; from here on she wasn't a girlfriend. The Wednesdays be-came Thursdays when Lucinda was at Zumba, and Zita was upgraded to mistress.

Although Zita lived alone and there was plenty of time and space for the interludes behind Lucinda's (toned) back, the question of Nigel's proclivity for fresh air remained. Which was why Zita was negotiating the budding country lanes and trying to tell a tale that spring Thursday evening.

What was it Nigel said? That's right: 'I think you'll find—'

Not that it mattered; he'd *interrupted*. Predictably interrupted again.

As the unexpected expletives bubbled out, Zita couldn't think of one single reason why she'd allowed him back in her life. She could only glare at this petty, inflated, self-opinionated little man and feel nothing but loathing. She hoped never to dirty her palms and her knees ever again. But there was a red-faced and gesticulating farmer in an orange tractor on her tail, and no-where to turn, so nothing could be done save to drive to the woodland carpark as planned.

Beetroot with outrage, Nigel stalked from the car and headed for trees. Watching the back of his neatly trimmed hair, Zita contemplated driving away, but she knew the rush of pleasure would be even shorter than a *petit mort*. And she'd be reprimanded, criticised and harried for days and weeks until his pique was spent. Far easier to follow him - eventually.

Where the heck was he? Inhaling the aroma

Hanged by the Neck

of damp earth and sour leaves, Zita roamed pathways carpeted with moss for a while. The forest was still and quiet - no Nigel, nor ramblers, not even a dog walker in sight. Picking her way across exposed tubers and fallen boughs, twisted ivy and knotweed, she finally headed towards the ravine. Save for the sound of her own breath and footfall, the silence was dense, the occasional piercing shriek or halloo of birds and small animals making her start. But as she neared the edge, the howl became human, the cry became her name. Falling to her knees, she crawled to the edge. Her body taut and hands trembling, she inched to the sound.

Hanging from the face of the gully by the sinewy stem of a tree, there was Nigel. His neat features were red and puffy, his eyes bulged, and the veins in his neck pulsated with the effort of holding on. The mass of sprouting green and purple foliage below was at least fifty feet.

'Zita. Help. Now,' he hissed.

Sandy orange soil was sprinkling his cheeks and invading his mouth. 'Quickly. Something to pull me up.'

Panting with alarm, she immediately stood and frantically turned to search the ground for a sturdy branch. Noticing the pulled root of a tree near the edge, Nigel's oft repeated words popped into her head. They now seemed rather funny.

'For the love of God, Zita, you don't have a disability. Lift your feet when you walk. You'll trip on a root and break your neck if you're not more careful.'

Turning back to the gorge, she peered over again. Poor Nigel. The spray of fine earth had become globular; a leak of small stones was escalating and the rhizome he clutched was slowly peeling from the clay.

Road signs flashed before her eyes. Stop! Weak Bridge! Give Way! Let alone the lectures, betrayal and, not least, the current debt...

Pulling a tissue from her pocket, she wiped her palms and knees for the very last time. Then she gave a little nod. 'Goodbye, Nigel. You know, you really should have just listened.'

Carefully obeying the speed limits on the way home, she contemplated whether Nigel had heard her final words. She hoped so. But his screaming had been rather loud.

Life *sans* Nigel on the Friday and over the weekend felt good. If Zita worried what Lucinda and her offspring were going through, she didn't dwell on it. She went to the library as usual, accepted compliments from her colleagues on how well she looked, smiled when they said yellow was really her colour and that 'whatever she was on', they'd like some. On the Monday she ate garlic bread with her pepperoni pizza for tea, she watched reality television for two hours with a tub of ice cream and settled in bed to read a trashy romance.

But Nigel came back.

The reprimands, the reproval and harrying went on all night, there in Zita's bedroom. Stunned

Hanged by the Neck

and confused, she didn't at first register the rotting smell. Nor the grime, the scratches and blood; the torn clothes and missing shoe; the displaced position of Nigel's shoulder, the protruding white knuckle of bone. Nor the spear of wood through his temple. But the penny finally dropped. The valedictory look on her lover's face was unmistakeable. She'd never get rid of him now.

Long days went by. Nigel's self-satisfied presence and his sniping were bad enough at home, but he'd turn up at the library to give a sneering commentary on the staff and the students, the books read and music borrowed. In the car too, appearing without warning to monitor her gear change and footwork. In the garden, in the bathroom, in the shower. Even at the supermarket - inspecting the contents of her trolly, keeping a tab on the calories.

On the plus side, Zita's house was tidy. But on the down, he was always there, watching her eat, censuring her nightwear selection, the television channel, choice of toothpaste or tights. Opining constantly. Following her through each room with the Hoover, dusting shelves, wiping fingerprints and rubbing smears from the granite, mirrors and glass.

The weeks of torment eventually became months, but little by little Nigel changed. He stopped visiting Zita at work. Or even in the car. He lost interest in surprising her at a window or on the loo. He kept his opinions to himself. He stayed at home and stared into space. Listless and vacant. Deflated, almost.

'What's wrong, Nigel?' Zita asked.

'I'm bored,' he replied.

She tried to help. 'What about watching daytime TV, Nigel? Or peeling the veg, getting rid of the dandelions, playing Cluedo or surfing the internet?'

The suggestions went on, but nothing would cheer him. Eventually bolstered by his passivity, she felt braver one day. 'Well, why don't you go off and haunt somebody else?'

His confession took some time, but finally came out. 'I can't,' he said reluctantly, 'I chose you.'

The rest of the saga soon followed. Poor Nigel. His body was stuck in the greenery at the bottom of the ravine. Spring had blossomed into summer and the foliage was thick, so no one had found it. He couldn't pass from this life to the next until it was discovered, blessed and buried. So he'd chosen to plague Zita. To punish her, of course. But she was the only one who could help. Ironic, wasn't it?

Nigel had to say please. Poor man. It was hard, very hard.

Steadily breathing out garlic that night, Zita contemplated her options. Should she tell Lucinda where Nigel used to walk? She wouldn't need to know Zita was there that day, though it would be fun to describe what went on in the woods and watch her double Ds quiver. But then again Lucinda was back at Zumba. She didn't seem so very sad without Nigel.

Could she call the police, an anonymous tip off? Or possibly go back herself and report a fishy smell?

Or perhaps... Sadly Nigel was no longer handsome and the stench was almost choking, but she was used to it now. And it was rather delicious to hear him beg. Besides, by wintertime the leaves would fall, the foliage become thin and his body might be found.

And if it wasn't, well, Nigel did love life *al fresco*.

LITTLE PIECE OF CHEER

Annie hangs her frayed nylon jacket on the peg. 'Mother, I'm home,' she calls. 'It's quite warm out there now.'

She looks at her palms. They're marked with deep grooves from the weight of the vegetables. Shrugging, she rummages in a carrier bag and carefully lifts out her treasure. A pot of perfect daffodils! The soil has spilt, exposing the onion-like bulbs to the world, but still they're her little piece of cheer.

'No bloody flowers!' Mother had shouted as Annie left to do the shopping. 'You know they make me sneeze.'

'Oh, Mother, a few flowers won't kill you,' she'd muttered in reply.

She now stares at the orange tipped trumpets. They're not flowers for the house, but a plant for the garden. Still, no point causing an argument; she'll hide them from Mother and see to them later.

Squeezing her tired eyes, she takes a hollow breath before entering the sitting room. Mother is crammed in her cosy chair by the electric bar heater, her fleshy arms folded.

'You look like a church candle, Annie. One that's dripping wax.'

'Well, it's roasting in here. You should turn off that fire.'

'And you should remember who's paying for it.'

Perching on the edge of a spindled chair, Annie unties her laces. The boots are from the catalogue and made of soft fabric, but they still chafe her ankles. She'll take the bus next time, Mother will never know.

'Are you going to comb your hair?' Mother asks. 'You look a sight.' The beetle eyes pierce her paunchy face. 'You never were a pretty girl, so all the more reason to take care of your appearance, Annie. No wonder you didn't get wed. Who'd have wanted you looking like you do? Now our Noreen, she was a beauty right from the start.'

'So you've told me, Mother. I'm putting on lunch.'

Leaning against the cooker, Annie sighs; she doesn't feel well, if truth be known, but there's no use moaning, she has Mother to care for, a hotpot to prepare. She scrubs the potatoes beneath the tap, then picks up the shallots, the celery and carrots, and shuffles to the table.

'I can see you're not at the sink,' Mother calls. 'You'll make a right mess, you will. It'll stain the wood. Have you laid newspaper on the table? Mind all the peelings go in the bin. Then I'll need changing.'

Annie shakes her head; she doesn't have the will to stand. Besides, there's nothing new to see from the kitchen window. Sixty-two years of staring at the top flat opposite, where Mother gave birth. 'Foreign holiday? I wish,' she joked with Beryl the neighbour. 'The furthest I've travelled is over this road.'

Pushing the door so Mother can't see, she skins the potatoes and carrots with a sharp paring knife, then cubes them like dice. The celery she chops, rat-a-tat-tat. But when it comes to the shallots, she cups them gently in her rough and sore hands, lost for moments in thought.

'I'll have another pot of tea and a slice of that fruit cake. You left it too long in the oven, but it'll have to do,' wafts through the crack in the door, but Annie isn't listening. She's unearthing the pot of daffodils, her little piece of cheer.

Still crammed in the cosy wingback, Mother wipes her plate clean with the crust of the bread. 'Noreen's stew has more flavour.' She nods to the photograph on the mantlepiece. 'What a bonny lass she is. That was taken just before you arrived to spoil things.'

'Oh, aye?' Annie retorts. 'And where's our Noreen now then? I don't see her waiting on you hand and foot, not like muggins here.'

'She's got better things to do with her time. She's a handsome husband and all those lovely

Hanged by the Neck

grandkids to love and spoil. Besides, she'll be up at Christmas, she's a good girl. Loves to see her old mum and collect her pressies.'

It's dusky outside. Mother's been sick again and she's calling from upstairs, but Annie is still gazing at the vase of cut daffodils. Turning to the kitchen door, she sees a small child. Thin, plain and solemn, she's carrying a skipping rope. 'Mother? Mother, I'm thirsty. Can I have a glass of water?' she's asking.

There's a woman at the floury table, pounding dough with her fists. She doesn't look up. 'You know where the tap is.' Then after a moment: 'I'll never love you,' she says. 'An unwanted little adulterine, that's what you are.'

The little girl flinches and the skipping rope falls, but she bites her bottom lip because she knows not to cry.

Lifting her head, the woman stares. 'There, I've said it,' she says with a firm nod, before resuming her chore.

'Annie love, are you all right? I was worried about you. I saw you come home from the hairdressers so I knew you were here, but when I knocked you didn't answer, so in I came.'

Annie opens her eyes to Beryl's troubled face. Alarm dances on her skin. 'Has something happened?' she asks. 'Is it Mother?' Her eyes sweeping the room, she takes in the cold electric heater, the empty cosy chair. 'Where's Mother?' she asks.

Her eyes teary, Beryl rubs Annie's hand. 'She's

in the hearse, love. Do you remember now? We're all waiting for you; it's time to go to church.' Though her chin wobbles with emotion, she tries for a smile. 'Never seen so many daffodils, love. They look cheery on the coffin, just like you said. Bet your mum would've been pleased. Come on, I'll help you to your feet. Oh look, these are beautiful shoes, Annie. I can see they're new.'

Annie slips in her feet. Black patent, lined in leather and so soft. Yes, she remembers now. A taxi ride into town yesterday. Manicure, lunch and a few shops. New shoes and a handbag, to match the cashmere coat.

She glances at the empty mantlepiece. 'Any word from our Noreen?'

Beryl shakes her head. 'Sorry, love, not a word. You'd think she'd have come today of all days.'

Checking her hair in the mirror, Annie pats it softly, pleased at what she sees. 'Well, our Noreen's got nothing to say bloody good riddance to, has she?' She gazes at Beryl's shocked face for a second. 'There I've said it,' she says with a firm nod.

A TROUBLE SHARED

A trouble shared. There's noise in this cafe, I know. Clinking and banging, coughing and laughter. But that's all I hear - the words, *a trouble shared*. It's what my Gran says. And it would be nice, so nice. But. Share a secret and you give a small piece of yourself away. Or perhaps a lot. Never tell if you don't want to be found out. Trust only yourself.

Remember your best friend in all the world when you were eight or nine? The one you told about peeing in the pool, writing on the toilet wall, even nicking a coin? Yeah, me too. Not her fault she let it out. Not anyone's. There's a compulsion, see. No point being told a secret without passing it on. Someone's shared this terrible tale and I'm shocked and smug and it makes me important. Powerful too. Like the slimy girl at school or at work, the one who's so friendly. The one who sidles up and flatters. So you open your mouth and you puke it all out. The thing you weren't going to tell. Not to anybody.

Rosalind, she was called. Long tresses that glowed

like the princess dolls' I was too old for, carefully hidden from Sharon beneath my bed. Spun gold. Her hair, high in its ponytail, was like that. Delicate treasure, sparkling in the sunshine and swinging from side to side.

She told me a secret.

Sometimes I'd like to tell mine. See if Gran's right. Just a bit 'cos it's lonely talking to myself. But then...

I've got mates, no problem, like now in this coffee shop. Talk to them all the time. Sometimes I'm pissed and I look at Tess or Chloe and I so nearly tell. So nearly spew out my guts. Get rid of the shit in my chest. But I don't. I won't, I really won't.

Come downstairs, Leah, love. There's a nice lady and a man who need to have a little chat with you.

That was my mum, eight years ago. A little chat? No one had *little chats* in our house. Everyone shouted. Or screamed. Or didn't talk at all.

Even now I can feel it - that clamp round my chest like a belt tied too tight as I crept down the stairs.

'You all right, Leah?' Tess's voice breaks through the sludge. Sounds of the busy cafe bounce back.

'Sorry, Tess? What did you say?'

There's a crease on her forehead. She nods at my mug. 'Your coffee's going cold. And look, Connor's over there. He's staring as usual. We're all flipping jealous, why don't you say yes?'

It's not that bad. Really, it isn't. Just sometimes it

gets me down. Start thinking about it and I can't stop. It scrambles my head. And I'm thinking and thinking in circles when I want to think straight. And I need to move on, but I'm stuck. So maybe if I told Tess. Just maybe.

I told on *her*. On Rosalind. Not until months later. I don't know why I finally did. Was *I* shocked and smug? Did *I* feel powerful or important? Perhaps. But after the accident, I couldn't sleep for thinking about it. Maybe that was it. So I told on her to Sharon.

    She was having one of those nice days, was my big sis. Asking about school and giving me her chocolate 'cos some boy had asked her out and she didn't want spots. The one day she didn't shout or say *disappear, pain, it was my room first*. So I told her what Rosalind had said. Watched her squint for mascara three times over in the mirror, then told her.

Guess what, Shaz? I know a secret.

There's a church on the way to work. Converted into flats. Luxury with stained glass windows. But still a church. And sometimes there's a blonde woman sitting on a bench in the garden and when my bus passes by, she looks up. Right at me.

I shake myself back to the warm room, Tess and her frown. Pick up my cup and down the coffee in one go. The caramel shot sticks to my molars. Wiping my top lip, I sigh. 'Don't go on about him, Tess.'

Then, 'Sorry, bit tired, that's all, didn't sleep.'

Tess cocks her head. 'Oh yeah?'

I stare at her face. It's open and friendly. Hear my Gran's voice - *a trouble shared*... 'Tess, have you ever been really...' I start, but Chloe's calling from the counter.

'Anyone fancy sharing a cake? Eclair or a vanilla?'

Tess scrapes back her chair. 'Let's have a look...'

'Have you ever wondered if...' I whisper again.

But Tess doesn't hear. Say it louder, much louder. We're grown ups now.

I clear my clotted throat. 'Tess? Can I ask you something?'

She turns. 'Yeah, sure, just give me a minute.'

I can't do it, of course. And it's fine, it really is. I don't need to tell. It's just when I'm on my own. The musty thoughts and what ifs. Beating me in. 'Specially when I'm bored. Nothing to do except feel lonely. But I look around the bubbling cafe and I know that's not true. I'm alone anyway. Like now. There's chat and music and noise and I'm looking at lips and teeth and gums, and without realising it's happened, I'm deaf like somebody's turned off the sound.

She breezed into year seven two weeks later than us. Rosalind. A new girl with hair that swung, catching the rays. Been living somewhere exotic before her parents split, was the rumour. Didn't like her

Hanged by the Neck

'cos I knew I wasn't her sort. Spoke posh and wore her uniform like it was fashion. Probably be top of the class, prom queen one day. But after a week she whispered to me, just me, as we waited for pizza in the dinner queue: *Hi there, I'm Rosalind.* Her pretty nose to the back of my greasy hair, so close to my ear. *But you can call me Rozzy.*

They used to put on a black cloth. On top the wig. Black gloves too. Before they said the words: *Hanged by the neck 'til ye be dead.* Or something like that. I saw it in a drama on the telly. That's what happens when I dream: the wig, the black cloth, the gloves; the wooden posts, the rope. The creaking of wood. Then a whooshing sound, followed by perfect silence. But that's not what happened. They don't sentence you to death these days. Her mother stood in that place, wearing her dressing gown. Pure silk, it was. She'd had her hair done, only that morning.

So I told on Rozzy. Sharon didn't even listen. Plastered on lipstick, did that smacking thing with her lips, sprayed perfume up her jumper, rummaged in a drawer. *Just in case,* she said with a grin. Flashed something square and shiny in the palm of her hand. Winked. *Just in case I score tonight.*

    She didn't even hear. That's what I thought.

'Want a bite, Leah? It's yum.'
    Tess is offering her cake. An eclair covered in sleek chocolate, the cream pulping out. Though I don't know if I can swallow, I take a small bite.

'Ta, Tess. Yeah, it's nice.'

I wrote it down once. On the back of a bus ticket. Tiny scrawl without gaps and when I ran out of space I wrote on top of the writing until the ticket crumpled into a mass of green sparkly gel. And without looking up, I knew someone was staring. So I scrunched it in the palm of my hand. Pretended to cough and I swallowed it.

Hey, Leah, fancy a swig? Rozzy asked one day in the playground. A bottle of coke; plastic, non diet. Her tanned smiling face watched mine as I took it. I didn't hesitate, or scrunch up my face. Drank greedily, give it back and turned, like a shrug.

Then her soft hand on my shoulder. *What do you think? Do you like it?*

'Course I wanted to cough 'cos it stung my throat, but I nodded as the heat crashed through my chest.

It's Julia's cherry brandy, she said. *Plenty more where this came from. Want another swig?*

So sometimes I get pissed. Really drunk or high in a pub or a club, and my head's spinning and I don't give a fuck. Not a care in the world. Everything's bloody hilarious. And then. Someone, something. Maybe a noise or a smell. God, I don't know. But I'm robbed sober. And that's when I start staring and seeing. Glimpses. Of her. Of nothing.

Special; I was special. Me and Rozzy were best mates. Hung out at school and the park, smoking her mum's ciggies, sometimes trying her stupid pills for a lark.

Julia's cigarettes, she'd say. *Have one, have a packet. Easy to nick. Money too. Alcohol, jewellery, whatever. Anything other than my bloody dinner.*

She called her mum Julia 'cos she knew how she hated it. *She's pathetic, is Julia, no wonder Dad left.*

Told me Julia was fearful of everything from spiders to illness, from loneliness to lies. Sobbed about anything: wrinkles and weight, grey hairs and grudges, sad stories, stray puppies. Would go out to buy bread or milk, but come back with clothes, or make-up or shoes. Bags and bags of stuff she'd already got.

Loves anything except me, Rozzy said, *perhaps I should burn them. And her.*

That's when she lit a match. I saw the flame in her eyes, but she laughed.

Don't look so serious, Leah, she's not that bad!

When the 'nice' lady and the man came, they were waiting in the back room with the glass door. But it was opaque, so you couldn't really see anything except outlines of dark colour around my homework table. I pushed it open by a finger. With shallow breaths, I stared, wondering what and why. Then I spotted Sharon examining her nails.

Sit down, Leah, the woman said in her *nice* voice. *We've come to ask you a few questions. About a friend of yours from school. Nothing to worry about. You're not in trouble. Take all the time you need.*

And Sharon was still staring at her hands.

Julia's own fault, really. That's what Rozzy's dad told her. On that hot April day she'd gone to the hairdressers, then when she came home, she'd put a pan on the gas, changed into a silk dressing gown and gone to bed with a bottle of gin. Mustn't have noticed the smoke, the smell of burning, of fire.

Rozzy, my Rozzy was inconsolable. *Do you think it was my dinner?* she asked.

I held her tightly, but God, how she cried.

She moved schools soon after, went to live with her dad. I travelled to her new home, just the once. Bunked off school, caught a bus and a coach. Tramped across fields to a huge mansion in the middle. Best and worst day of my life. We echoed through the house, room by room, drunk on daring and far more than cherry brandy. Feasted on food, smoked cigars; stripped and smooched to soft music.

That day Rozzy loved me, let me touch her smooth skin, let me stroke her silky hair. But that's when she told me. Cupping me from behind, her breath hot on my cheek. *Remember what I said about matches? Never touch?* she asked. And I was still lost in desire when she spoke again: *Shall I tell you another secret?*

Tess taps my shoulder, bringing me back. 'Leah, look. Connor's coming over. He's so bloody good looking. You can't not say yes.'

'I'm not really—'

'But he likes you, Leah. He really does. And it isn't as though there's been anyone else you've really fancied.'

Eight years ago today; like a life sentence served. But the guilt's still there. Regret too. I betrayed the only person I ever loved.

Rosalind, Rosalind. You should never have told me your secret. Not the one about your mum and matches, but the other - the handsome boy from your new school, the blow-by-blow account of what you'd both *done,* your new love *forever.*

The bad stuff comes in waves, without being asked, but there's still that feeling, bitter sweet. A clenching sensation. One that makes my cheeks burn and my chest ache. A cafe's a good place to share a trouble, but that's the one secret I'll never give away.

Not to anyone.

THE DELIVERY

Tidy my hair, you say clearly from the back seat of my cab.

You give me a start; I didn't expect you to talk.

You look at me expectantly through eyes backlit by blindness. *Now be careful, young man, I want to look my best when I arrive.*

You lean your small sunken face towards me, the papery skin decorated with affectionate fluff.

Go on, I won't bite, you say with a smile.

So I comb your feathery hair with my fingers. Thick, clumsy and sticky with sweat, I'm afraid it will come away in my hands. You frighten me with your fragility, a bag of fleshless bones, dressed in your best for a wedding.

You speak as I drive, your voice scented with time.

I'm in winter now, you say. *My branches are stripped clean and I'm preparing to die. Sans everything.*

But it wasn't always that way.

You smile a wistful smile. *Well, we all start at childhood...*

How far back can you go? Not as far as you

should. It's the smell you remember. The dank of the dark closet, fusty fox fur and sour mothballs; starched linen, old shoes. Then the scrape of a key and the shrill in her voice.

You hesitate then. *The fear never went away. All alone. For hours...*

A barren aunt, you explain. Older brothers and sisters aplenty at home, but you were the one *given away* to your uncle's wife.

Empty in heart and soul as well as in womb, she was, you add with a sigh.

Not the love of a child your aunt had desired, but help around her large creaking house, an unpaid and unloved maid, dressed like a doll.

Turning your face to the window, you sniff. *Mother, father and the boys; Joyce, Annie and Ethel; I missed them so much. How I longed to go home...*

You fall into silence and I drive, relieved to return to my own troublesome thoughts - small irritations about money and work, a love affair gone stale, the need for a new jacket and repairs to the car, but a sudden squall batters the roof and you continue to chat.

Still it wasn't so bad, you say.

Endless fresh countryside, Mary Jane shoes, pretty frocks and rules in an accent you didn't understand until you were broken, then mended and became one of them. Though you still mourned for home, you were contented then. Smelling of poverty and grass, the local kids knocked at your aunt's back door, asking you to play in a dialect you now understood.

I still taste it, you say with a smile. Clover and bilberries, liberation and laughter among the bracken hills.

Then one day you returned dirty, your fine clothes soiled with happy grime. That was the first time you were sent to the wardrobe. After that, its murky depths became a daily dose for even the smallest offence.

You lift your knotted hands to the heavens. *Then the miracle happened*, you say with a smile.

A fresh little cousin, baked and born unexpectedly. Now surplus to requirements, you were returned to sender.

Home at last, you say.

But you were a strange little packet. Afraid of the dark, you were a delivery no one knew or understood, not even your mother. And so, for a time, you were friendless again, a single narcissus in a crowd of urban daffodils, buffeted gently by April showers.

Your sudden grin lights the cab. *Bright as a berry*, you say, *that's what the school said!*

At eleven years of age, warmth came with the autumn. Plucked by a teacher, you were the honour of the family then, wearing your grammar school uniform with pride. Your eager brothers echoed, but they went to war.

The beam falls from your lips; your eyes fill with pain. *Forever to war,* you say. Jimmy, John and Fred. Skinny legs, ginger freckles, bashful smiles. The tears of a father who never cried. A mother's look of tired resignation.

A terrible waste, too young, too young. Far too young to die.

Then you laugh and hum a tune. *And of course the summer of love!*

As fresh as the flowers, the melody still soft in your head, a dance that went on forever and was sealed with a kiss. Your Harry, no one else's, so you lifted your petticoat and said yes.

The shame came soon after, the family pride dented forever, you thought. But your mother smiled sadly. Many a spillage betwixt cup and lip and what did it matter anyway when so many were dead, we must all live for today, she said.

So the bans were read, invitations sent. In a borrowed grey suit, Harry clasped your hand at the altar. Your mother and sisters smiled with shiny eyes, but your father didn't move from the doors. Waiting, still waiting for his sons to arrive, *better late than never*.

I gaze through the spattered windscreen and will on your tale. You don't keep me waiting for long.

Motherhood, you say, the pleasure laced in your voice. The part you loved the best.

Happy, so happy, your life filled with joy. Two girls, born eleven months apart; similar in looks, yet so different in character. Both delivered at home with only your mother for company and a rag for the pain.

Then eventually your boy, your lovely boy.

He came so quickly, so eager to come out, a perfect smooth-skinned child who'd *been here before*. He never cried, your Michael. He simply watched with knowing eyes until the day he died. In front of the fire, then a fit and he was gone, *the coffin the size of a ruler.*

Pulling up at red lights, I gaze through the mirror. You've covered your face with shaking fingers. *The weather changed*, you whisper.

Joy turned to fear. A dark depression Harry couldn't lift, a good man gone bad, too much ale and work, too much to bear. He left you frightened by black moods and fists, until eventually he left you completely, strung up in the attic, then buried with his son.

Taking a deep breath, you lift your small chin. *No money,* you say. *Food and heating, clothes and rent.* Down to you now, the grammar school girl. No longer just Mummy; you finally became Mary.

You chuckle and I smile with relief. How you enjoyed your working days at the Solicitor's office. Friends for life in the typing pool, your own pay packet and a sense of worth; chatter and camaraderie before dashing home on the bus to prepare tea for the girls. Time blew by, the days became weeks and the weeks turned to years. The girls grew into bright young women with lives of their own.

You frown and shake your head. *History repeated itself*, you say, *as only history can.*

With a crestfallen face, Barbara came home to confess. A grandmother in waiting, you tried to remember the words your own mother had used. Life is too short, you tried to say, but there wasn't a Harry in the wings for Barbara, no one to wed in too-short trousers, just a lonely attempt at birth in a hospital.

Complications, you say, *both mother and son lost. But together, like home.*

Then your lovely Margaret, your first born. She didn't want to marry, so she stayed with you, in unison, inseparable, like *conkers in a shell.*

The autumn of contentment and easy companionship, baking and walks, gardening and church. Until one dark day she came home and said there was something... And it was spreading, too late to treat, her body riddled, they said.

But you were there, tending and loving until the very end.

Your children, your children, your beautiful children. *They went home before me. It wasn't the natural order*, you say, *but who was I to question why?*

The new sun warms the car. Sighing, you close eyes and smile softly. *But I was lucky, it was a good life*, you say, as sleep pulls you in.

Chastened by my own petty worries and concerns, I nod and drive on.

When we reach our destination, I stop the meter and turn. For a moment I gaze. I don't need to wake you; your eyes are closed but I'm certain the illumination has gone.

Though I wipe the tears from my cheeks, I smile. Arms have reached out to take you home, and

Caroline England

I'm so glad you looked your best when you arrived.

GONE IN AN INSTANT

'I hope she likes it. I wasn't sure what to bring her. I mean, I know it's all digital these days, but she's still so young, and having no kids... Well, I wasn't sure what she'd like.'

'It's perfect,' I assured her. 'She'll have fun with it, I promise.'

I had waited for Jolene's arrival with folded arms. She was Dave's cousin, not mine, and six whole weeks was a long time, even if she was recently widowed. Indeed, I built up her stay to gargantuan proportions. How would I entertain a stranger all day? What types of food would she eat? Being a new mum was full on - when would I get time to myself? And more to the point in our small cottage, where would she sleep?

Dave shrugged as he always did. It'll be fine; she's great. I'll take days off work, Bryony will love her, you'll love her; she'll stay some of the time with the family, and so on, until his reasonable platitudes made me feel mean-spirited. It was the least I could do for him, and of course my only child. Jolene was Dave's Canadian cousin, and though Bryony wasn't our biological daughter, Jolene was her family too.

Naturally I'd heard about the Ontario connection. Covered in thick protective wax, the huge Canadian cheese arrived in the post each Christmas like clockwork. The romance was fairytale; Jolene's mother had been a war bride, whisked off her feet by a handsome foreign airman who turned out to be the heir to a chain of pharmacies in Toronto. Dave and his brothers had visited there as children, spending long weeks in the summer with their cousins, hanging out with the local kids and having a riot. Such were their rose-tinted memories that the same slide show was shown on our white dining room wall each Boxing Day. Repeated snapshots of Dave, Andy and Mike with their cousins and a host of other young people only they could name, camping, boating, climbing or swimming. With huge grins, hilarious laughter and hugs, they were clearly having fun. I wished I could have recognised similar images from my own childhood, but I was the only one, and solitary at that.

Dave and his brothers didn't tire of the same photographs every time, nor did they notice the wives' discreet bored withdrawal. We may not have particularly warmed to each other, but it was the one occasion we had a united front. None of us liked the invasion of the Canadian contingent, even if it was only by Polaroid.

I suppose the joyful snaps influenced me. Save for being female, would Jolene and I have anything in common at all? I expected her to be loud, beautiful, brash and opinionated. I anticipated total unwelcome invasion into my happy little world, our happy little world, Dave, Bryony and me. It had taken so long to create that I was fearful of an impostor upsetting its fragile balance.

Jolene finally arrived mid-July. Far from the imagined spectre, I liked her the moment she walked into my home. Small and quiet, she was devoid of make up, and her brown eyes were soft and warm; they immediately drew me in, making me feel assured and comfortable. And instead of imposing or disrupting, she seemed to slot in with the rhythm of our lives during that slow dank summer.

Bryony loved her too. 'Another photograph Auntie Jolene?' she'd ask, the disposable camera held at a rakish angle, her small thumb almost obscuring the lens. 'Oh, don't waste your photographs on me, honey. Take a snap of your gorgeous, beautiful mom,' she'd laugh.

And the amazing thing was that I *felt* it. How Jolene did it, I had no idea, but she had a knack of making me feel just that - gorgeous, beautiful - special.

Bryony and I wept when she left, and even Dave looked wistful. We'd had such a lovely summer, despite the almost constant drizzle. Jolene had taught Bryony to crochet and I rediscovered my art, spending far too much time in the rain-drenched fields beyond the cottage, drawing and painting all day, coming home hungry and late, but feeling incredible. I had gone back to *creating* through my own endeavours, something my failure to conceive had all but destroyed.

Far from the claustrophobia I had dreaded, Jolene's stay gave me freedom from the self-imposed rigour of new motherhood. By releasing that fearful grip, I found the person I was before the crippling diagnosis of being hollow, an empty vassal, a failure.

When together in the cottage, our amiable silences had been so comfortable, we didn't talk as much as one might imagine. Indeed, our subsequent correspondence was more informative than our daily rubbing of shoulders at the kitchen sink.

I already knew that Jolene was widowed, her childhood sweetheart dead at the wheel of his car, but she didn't raise it or offer how she felt, so I didn't pry. Her desire for a child was unspoken but loud; I could see it from her interaction with Bryony, the way she gazed at her small face etched with concentration as she focused on another stitch. And of course I recognised the yearning, a burning echo of how I had felt for so long. It was an unspoken empathy, but one I felt was communicated through support, touch and easy companionship. Distance inevitably removed the intimacy, but it was replaced, not by talking on the telephone, but by the written word.

'Guess what,' Jolene penned in the autumn. 'You know that old flame I wrote about? Well, one thing led to another, as they say and...drum roll...I'm pregnant! Having a scan next week to find out how far gone I am. Will you let the guys know? I can't tell you how thrilled I am...'

We were all excited. If there was just a flash of green from me, it wasn't because I was jealous of the ease with which Jolene had fallen pregnant, but that I hadn't known without being told. Silly though it was, I was disappointed with the failure of my own intuition; my relationship with Jolene was so finely tuned that I had expected some kind of advanced warning of such momentous news. Still, I was pleased for my friend, and Bryony and I took to the shops with a mission. We sat amongst the early Christmas decorations in the department store café, exhausted from our endeavours to buy gifts in neither blue nor pink, ones which would suit whichever season the baby might be born.

Revived by her muffin and a milkshake, Bryony took an excited deep breath and picked up the wallet of photographs we'd collected from the photo lab earlier that day. She had lost interest in the camera after Jolene left, but it had finally been used up on Halloween.

She flicked through the top of the pile. 'It wasn't the same without Jolene,' she said, discarding dark and badly focused snaps of the party table and pumpkin. She slowed as she gazed at the summer, its reflection bright in her eyes.

She turned with a luminous smile. 'The picnic, Mummy! Do you remember?' she asked. 'It was such fun.'

Taking the photograph, I smiled at the memory. It had been August Bank holiday, the one day that it hadn't threatened to rain. All Dave's family had come, each contributing a different item of food, from sausage rolls to sardines, couscous, cucumber and cherries. From strawberries to tomatoes and Turkish figs. And of course champagne, far too much champagne.

As though poor-sighted, I brought the picture closer to my eyes. It was focused on Jolene laughing at the lens, her hand lifted as though to stop the instant. Dave was by her side, not looking at the camera, but at her, a gaze I immediately recognised, but one I hadn't seen for a long time.

Snaps of the summer flashed through my mind. Hints I had seen but been blind to. The stab of certainty took my breath. 'A spring baby,' I said out loud. 'Jolene's baby will be born in the spring.'

WASTED TIME

I watched the boy through the rain-smeared bay. At his nan's front door, he was kicking the grit, his angelic face looking glum. Fair hair plastered to his head, he stared across the street, at the cat, then at me. Waited until he caught my eye, then he lifted his hand, his fingers signing an expletive.

'Nan says you're a waste of fucking space,' he shouted.

'How would you describe it, then?'

I don't like the man. He has that way of raising his eyebrows and sighing; he's patronising me, and I'm playing into his hands because I'm distracted by the woman sitting at his side. She hasn't introduced herself, but she sits there, gazing at me and biting the inside of her mouth, just below her greasy lips.

'The punch; the punch to the old lady's face. How would you describe it, then?' he repeats, eyebrows raised and sigh at the ready.

The chalk seemed luminous against the damp. It was early. His strawberry-blonde fringe flopped over his brow as he scrawled on the pavement.

Cripple, I read.

Lifting his head to the window, he started with surprise when he saw me. He smiled, his front teeth slightly askew, then he crouched again.

Fucking cripple, I read, as he sauntered away.

I try to focus on the man. He's tanned, far too tawny for a cold December morning. And he wears a signet ring, large and vulgar on a too-slender finger.

'I don't know,' I say. 'It looked like a play punch to me. It's what you'd expect from a... I don't know, ten, eleven year old boy? It looked like he was just mucking around, being daft.'

Tan man looks disappointed. You've let me down, his look says. You can do better than that.

'He'll be twelve next week,' he says, as though I should have the bloody date on my calendar.

The dull thud of the football against the bay woke me again, third time that week. I didn't need to peep through the curtains to know it was the boy, but I couldn't resist.

'So, when was this exactly?' the man asks. He digs into his pocket and takes out a notebook. Looks at me and sighs before wetting his finger with a pointed tongue to turn the page.

'A week ago?' I answer.

The woman moves onto her thumb, but continues to stare. The Christmas tree lights from number eleven catch my gaze as I wrench it from her face.

'Can't we do better than that, Mr Greenhill?' Tan man again, still looking let down.

I ruffle what's left of my hair and smile apologetically. 'I'm not exactly sure,' I tell them. 'I saw the boy through the window at some point last week. He was with his nan, Betty Yates.'

Tan man waits for more.

'It was snowing,' I say. 'They were leaving the house and he threw a punch. That's all I know.'

'Is he friendly? Your cat.'

The boy nodded at my bay window sill, his blue eyes bright with yearning. 'Can I come in and stroke it?' he asked. He turned and squinted against the winter sunshine. 'My nan hates cats.'

'Look, we've got a missing child. Right across from where you live. Now I know you've got problems with...your mobility...'

He's condescending me again, speaking slowly and casting glances at the woman, pointed looks I'm too old or too stupid to see.

'...but, we need to be as clear about everything as possible. Are you following me?'

'What happened, then?' I ask. 'Where's the boy gone?'

'That's what we're here to find out, sir. Now, you were telling us about the punch.'

The boy knelt on the floor, holding a wafer in one hand and stroking the cat with the other. The pussy purred, pushing its warm body against his gentle touch and I watched, unable to tear my eyes away from the boy's features - his turned-up nose and freckled cheeks, the shade of his hair, the fullness of his mouth.

'Can I have another biscuit?' he asked.

Audrey hacks for several moments, then croaks through the privet. 'No one's heard anything all day. Looks like that boy's still missing.'

I can see the movement of her lips through a tiny gap in the leaves. I had let the bush grow higher than either of us, but she's too dim to take the hint.

'Wonder what's happened to him, poor lad,' she shouts from her side. 'Bit of a trouble-maker, though. Why he moved in with his nan, I expect. Teach him a bit of discipline, Betty Yates would. Mind you, he's probably the reason why she had that angina attack. Police come round to yours as well?'

She knows the answer well enough. Probably had to turn the television down for once.

'Did you see his mam was on the local TV? Looked worried sick, though she hasn't half put weight on since she lived round here. I've told my Nancy—'

But I stop listening and close the back door.

Joanne Yates. Closing my eyes, I picture her. Right from the start she was the sort of kid you couldn't take your gaze off. A real pearl; all skippy and smiley.

'Hiya, Mr Greenhill, can I come in and see your cat?' she'd call from over the road.

Course, she'd soon be fetched in by a frown from her mother. But later she'd knock on the door for a handful of mint imperials when her mam had a nap.

She grew up in no time and left home to get wed. But still she rapped on her mam's door every second Sunday. She was expecting and then nothing. The visits stopped. They must have had words, her and Betty, words that lasted until the young lad appeared.

He stood behind me at the bay. Betty was shouting his name from her garden gate. Wearing slippers and a housecoat, her face was contorted.

'If she was dead, I could live here, couldn't I?' the boy asked. 'My mam doesn't want me. Not any more. She only loves him and the baby. So I could live here and you'd look after me.'

Three doorbell peals, each longer than the last. I can see her distorted face through the frosted glass. She's an impatient bitch, so I take my time.

'Mr Greenhill, can I have a word? DI Barnes. Remember, from yesterday?' she says through the postbox.

So, she has a voice after all. And thinks I'm deaf.

'The boy still hasn't been found,' she yells. 'We need to go over what happened again. Can you open the door?'

I watched as the ambulance silently winked. They

brought her out on a stretcher, immobile. Betty Yates, the old cow. Hadn't spoken to her for well over twenty years. Longer probably. Not since she knocked on and accused me of dumping rubbish on the common at the end of the road.

'You're the only thing that's common round here,' I had replied.

'Oh, aye. Jealous are you?' she'd fired back.

My God, she'd aged badly close up. Rolls of flesh around her midriff and chins to match. No wonder she hadn't married, given her Joanne a dad.

I'd wanted to say she'd been around the blocks a few times too many for me to care a brass farthing, but I wasn't going to waste my breath.

'What about the boy's mother. Joanne, isn't it?' I ask DI Barnes. 'She used to live 'round here. Is she all right? She's just had a new baby, hasn't she?'

She does the usual with her mouth. It must be sore, I think, as I admire the extravagant angel at the top of my Christmas tree.

Edging towards me, the detective stares with cold eyes. 'A new baby, eh? Now how on earth do you know that?'

I take a windy breath. 'It must have been on the news. The local news or in the paper. Or perhaps she just looked tired and I guessed. Maybe Audrey told me. That must have been it. Yes, Audrey, my neighbour. Saying that the girl had put on weight and I put two and two together.'

'That right?' She moves onto her thumb.

'You're looking a bit peaky. You all right, Mr Greenhill?'

The woman nods slowly. Says nothing but squints at the stairs over my shoulder.

'Did you ever settle down or have kids, Mr Greenhill?' she eventually asks.

As he napped, I touched his face. He looked so young, felt so warm. My fingers were trembling and I was afraid that he'd wake and be frightened, but when his blue eyes opened, he looked at me intently.

'Is it Nan? Is she dead?' he asked. 'I'm not going back. I hate her. I can stay, can't I?'

And I steadied myself to tell him the truth. I sat on the bed and took a deep breath. 'Look...' I began.

But he reached out his soft hand and laid it on mine. 'Please. I'll be good, really good. I promise. I can stay, can't I? Just for a bit? I'll feed the cat and put on the kettle. Please say yes.'

And I nodded.

'Live on your own. Never been married. No kids. Bit of a recluse. Armchair facing the window, not the TV. What do you get up to all day, Mr Greenhill? Must be something that rings your bell.'

The woman's stopped chewing and she's looking right at me, just like she knows what's inside.

'I'll go if you want me to,' he said in the morning.

He licked his lips and his entreating eyes held mine. 'But you said I could help decorate the Christmas tree. You promised. It'll look great, it really will.' He rested his cheek against my rough skin. 'Don't you like me being here? I thought we were friends.'

'You should go to your mam, you know. Call her at least. Worried sick, she'll be. She was on the news. You really should,' I said.

I tried my hardest, I really did, but the boy knew it was just words and I couldn't let go.

'Like watching, do you, Mr Greenhill? The kids in the street? The skipping, the giggling, the football? Remind you of your happy childhood, eh?'

She's glaring and pacing, making my head spin.

'Or maybe it's something else. Make you feel nice do they? Blushing little girls. Or maybe just boys? Is that what you like? Young boys. Pretty boys with blonde hair? Like our missing lad...'

'You let me think she was dead. I've seen her, my nan. You lied. You fucking liar. I hate you. I hate you. I hate you.'

But he didn't run. He grabbed my flannel shirt tight in his fists. Then he sobbed.

'Don't make me go back. Please don't make me.'

'Disability living allowance, eh?' There's a sneer in her voice. 'Heard that one a few times before.

Friendly doctor's all it takes, some say. Better give me his name then.' She nods towards the stairs. 'So, it's arthritis, is it? Covers a multitude of sins does arthritis. Let's have a look at your pills, shall we? Up there, I'm guessing. You lead the way Mr Greenhill. Take your time.'

'There's something I want to show you,' I said to the boy. 'A little surprise. But it's up in the attic. You'll have to fetch it for me. Just climb up the ladder. Don't be afraid...'

Disturbed earth beyond the cherry, DI Barnes said, so they're digging. Her arms folded, she gnaws away and watches a whole team of officers in white from the kitchen window.

I sit at the bay and wait for Betty to come over.

His head touched mine as we gazed at the photographs. The fusty smell of wasted time caught my throat and burned my eyes; my swollen knuckles ached with my heart as I flipped the worn pages.

I turned to watch him. 'Who's that then?' I asked, pointing.

He gazed at the black and white snap, then he traced the boy's face with his finger. The turned up nose, cherubic smile, the plump freckled cheeks.

Looking up at me, his features creased in confusion. 'It says Billy Greenhill, aged ten. But he looks just like me,' he replied.

Betty takes her time, but finally she comes over

with a face like thunder and raps at my door. Mourning the beauty I once loved, I gaze for a moment, searching to find a glimpse of her beneath the anger and puffy skin.

'Let's see it then.'

She stares at the photograph, then nods. And though she spits out the words, they're like a blessing from heaven.

'You. Bloody typical. Must've needed my eyes testing.'

Though I should have known; a real pearl she was; all skippy and smiley, my girl.

A REMINDER OF SIN

She couldn't describe the pain to me nor the doctors, save to say it was like severe labour pains, only worse because there was no let up at all - a searing spasm which lasted for hours some months, for days in others. I cared for her the best that I could, and there were times when I caught a glimpse of the girl she once was, the stunning, smiling, vivacious woman I had befriended. But with a face etched with pain, she no longer looked like her. She had test after test at the beginning, but the medics could find nothing wrong physically, so she gave in, not only to them, but to the curse.

Daphne and I had been friends since third year university. I hadn't liked her for the first two. I had observed her from a distance and I knew she wasn't my sort: too loud, too polished, too popular. And inevitably, too beautiful. Everyone wanted a piece of her, which was why I always held back, even when we became the last two survivors in Mr Latona's Greek tutorial group.

'Do you think it's the stutter?' she asked, looking around the empty room on the third week. 'I rather like it. I find myself anticipating the next word and feeling very clever when I get it right.'

I couldn't help but smile; I'd been thinking along those lines myself.

'Or maybe it's because he's so bloody boring,' Daphne added. 'It's Diana, isn't it? Why are we still here, Diana? Come on; time to escape before he arrives.'

'Do you like it when a man goes down on you?'

Those were Daphne's first words when we finally found an empty table in the refectory. I didn't get chance to reply. 'Or, perhaps, a woman?' she asked. Twisting her silky mane, she studied me with her startling blue eyes. 'I haven't decided.'

'Decided...?'

'That would be telling!' she replied, helping herself to the chips on my plate.

That was Daphne for you. I could never quite pin her down. Sometimes she'd regale me with too much information about her sexual exploits, at other times it was difficult to see through her fog of hint and innuendo. On this occasion, like many others, I wasn't entirely sure what she was saying, but it didn't matter. Out of nowhere I was wanted. By Daphne Callisto, of all people. Like hurtling into a warm summer gale, it was exhilarating.

Daphne met Adrian on her first day as a trainee at Janus and Son. She knew it was a terrible cliché, but she said it to me nonetheless, hours after they had been introduced.

'He's the one, Diana. I'm sure of it.'

'The wealthy boss's son, Daphne, how predictable,' I replied. 'And besides, if he's already married, isn't that going to be a little tricky?'

Save for a determined set of her chin, Daphne's face was calm. I hadn't seen her this way before and I felt a pang of loss. She was usually so animated and flippant, her enthusiasm for one lover merging with the next, so her reply surprised me.

'No, Adrian was married but she died. Not long ago, apparently, so I'll have to tread carefully with this one.'

A little time passed and Daphne *trod as carefully* as she knew how.

'Gloria's a witch. No really, Diana, the woman's a witch, a real witch, there's no doubt about it,' she declared when we next met.

I laughed at her usual hyperbole. 'And you know this how?' I replied. 'Found her book of spells in the cupboard with the Dresden?'

'Really, Diana, I'm serious. It's the eyes.' She looked at me with a troubled frown. 'There's something strange about her. She doesn't like me.'

'Strange indeed,' I replied, and it struck me for the first time that Daphne wasn't used to being disliked.

Almost on the verge of tears, she looked pensive, so I put my arms around her and pulled her close. 'Come on Daphne. She's only human,' I said. 'Don't you think being *up the duff* by her recently widowed son has something to do with it?'

I finally met Gloria at her first grandson's christening. Taller, glamorous, much younger than I expected. Not a crooked nose nor a stoop in sight.

'You've met her then,' Daphne whispered as she chopped tomatoes with surprising ferocity. 'I think she left her broomstick at home today. She's almost being nice, but don't let that fool you.' She flung her arms around my shoulders and held on to me tightly. 'Thank God you're here. You're my number one!' She kissed my cheek and smiled. 'Save for Adrian, obviously.'

I met Gloria again at the following two baptisms. I thought she was pleasant, in a *lady bountiful* type of way. Each time she wore a wide brimmed hat which partially hid her face, so it was difficult to gain eye contact, but she was tactile, brushing my shoulder as I bent to kiss her cheek, then linking her arm through mine as we strolled through the gardens.

I was impressed; she remembered everything I had told her at the previous christening. Which was, in fact, too much. I didn't generally talk for so long, not about myself anyway, and it was flattering to have such copious attention, tremendously so. It wasn't until the third christening that the penny dropped - the information she was extracting wasn't really about me.

'Oh, different fathers, of course.'

It was Daphne's stock reply when people commented on how dissimilar the three boys looked. And they did appear different at first glance, though all shared the Janus nasal intonation and blue hooded eyes.

Typical Daphne, of course. She still liked to see the moment of confusion and hesitation before realisation dawned that it was her idea of a joke. Her teasing always seemed incongruous, considering her own gullibility, but it was nice to see the old Daphne back after her sons were pelted out in rapid succession. It was lovely to see that vivacious girl again.

I had been through her pregnancies step by step, almost from conception to birth and each stage in between, holding her hand when Adrian was absent, so I immediately knew from her pasty face she was expecting again.

'Bloody hell, Daphne - you're up the duff again, aren't you?'

She nodded, but said nothing.

Though I had been away for a few weeks, I was disappointed she hadn't confided in me. 'That's great news,' I said carefully. 'You love babies. You are pleased, aren't you?'

Dropping her gaze, she shook her head and I instinctively knew why she'd kept the news to herself.

'Well, I guess Adrian doesn't need to know...'

I said slowly, battling to keep the strange heave of emotion from showing.

Daphne shrugged and looked away. 'Suppose the baby has brown eyes, what then?' she asked.

Brown eyes didn't matter in the end.

As soon as I heard, I hurried to the hospital. Glancing around the ward I saw mothers and their babies, tired fathers and bored kids, grandmas arranging flowers, but no Adrian nor Gloria.

'Oh Daphne! How bloody insensitive of the staff, putting you in here.'

The words came out too loudly, but I was angry for her because she had no energy to be indignant for herself.

When she rocked her head towards me, her eyes were empty. 'Gloria knew, you know.'

'Knew what?'

'About the baby's brown eyes. She told me a story. Just before...this. About a curse, infidelity. I wasn't really listening.'

'Oh, Daphne. You're just upset. You've been through a terrible ordeal but it's over. You'll get better with time. Maybe try for another.'

Daphne's voice was hoarse. 'I wasn't really listening because she scared me, Diana. She looked at me with those black eyes and I thought of the first wife. How did she die? Does anyone know? And the curse; she said it lasted as long as one could bear children. Every month, a reminder of sin, she said. So maybe it isn't over.'

I almost snorted then, wanted to say it was rubbish, that it sounded very much like a description of every woman's curse - menstruation - but she interrupted, her face solemn. 'Diana, please just listen. I'm scared, really scared. I'm too frightened to go home. Can I come and live with you? Money won't be a problem, I still have Daddy's money...'

I was needed. By Daphne Callisto, of all people. So I pulled back from my laughter and took her soft hand in mine. 'Yes, absolutely. Of course you can.'

I met Gloria for the final time at Daphne's funeral. She didn't wear a hat, but as I might have expected, her eyes were hidden by huge sunglasses. There were surprisingly few people, considering how loved Daphne had been through the years. Her tearless boys stood by their father, hands behind their backs, as the coffin was lowered into the ground. They looked comfortable in their pin-stripe suits, Sons in the making for the Janus brand.

Gloria slipped her arm through mine as we strolled from the grave. She glanced at me with a smile.

'We have so much in common, we must keep in touch,' she said. 'Love and hate, it's a fine line,' she added, wafting a wasp with a leather-gloved hand. 'Daphne used to call me a witch, you know. She thought I could read her mind and cast spells. Which is ridiculous, of course.'

We continued our saunter to the car park. A

chauffeur stood by the open door of the Bentley. Gloria stepped elegantly into the back seat. 'Money can buy many things, but the power of suggestion should never be underrated,' she said, removing her shades.

Large pupils were set in fine blue eyes, I noticed, but nothing more sinister.

'But you knew that already, didn't you?' she continued. 'Unrequited love's a terrible thing, I believe, betrayal even worse.' She broke the gaze with a blink and slipped on her sunglasses. 'But you got what you wanted, darling; we both did.'

I didn't miss a beat. 'Gloria, I have no idea what you're talking about.'

Climbing into my Mercedes, I settled in the leather seat and inhaled the unique smell of new car. I nodded and smiled, then finally I closed the door with a satisfying thud.

GODLINESS

Folk buy anything, and not just the people you'd expect, the destitute and decayed. The students come, of course, with their torn jeans and twenty pound notes, but so do workers, freaky mums and their snotty kids. As Flora would say, so long as it's a bargain, everything sells. Except gloves; no one wants to buy them. They sit in a basket by the counter. More often than not, they're not even a pair, just one sad old lonely glove, waiting for a reason.

I shave and shower as soon as I get home to get rid of the smell.

'I see you're still using that new fangled bloody spout,' Mother says from the front room, her fat arse crammed into the wing backed chair, just as I left her this morning. 'Waste of money and you won't get clean, not properly clean.'

'Don't worry, the water will be hot...' I reply, counting the stairs. Two, four, six...even numbers up, odd numbers down.

Bloody parrots we are. We've learnt our lines good and proper, Mother and me, but we rub along.

'A really good scrub. And make sure you put the curtain inside the tray...' I mouth as the shrill of her voice follows me up.

I was lost once. Had my head down, counting the risers on the escalator, losing score as they flattened out at the top. When I looked up, she'd gone. Mother, that is. I can remember the panic, even now. It rose from my toes to my face, then dropped again like a dead weight to my feet, rooting me to the spot.

I scanned the store floor, searching for her thick ankles, but they all looked the same. Winter coats buffeted me as people struggled to get by. Then someone gave me a shove and I stumbled to my bare bony knees. When I picked myself up, a man moved to one side and there she was, my mother, holding out her palm towards me and smiling, just like she meant it.

'Come on, love,' she said. 'Did you lose me?'

And I took it, her hand, feeling the steel of those plumped up fingers as she nodded goodbye to a woman from church.

An old Crombie coat came in to the shop, one that didn't stink, for once. It was in perfect condition, lined with deep maroon silk and I couldn't resist, not when Flora said it would be a perfect fit for a gent like me. She laughed as I gave her a twirl. And deep in a pocket I found a glove, dark brown leather, almost black, supple and expensive. A real man's glove. So I slipped it on, savouring the feel of the soft lining against my fingers.

'Doctor says chronic eczema,' Mother would say if

anyone was curious, but no one asked, not much anyway. Just the kids at school, and I was used to them.

Standing at the glass, the sharp night air catches the back of my throat.

'Close that bloody window,' I hear, or so I think. If she hasn't said it yet, she will soon enough.

'All right, all right,' I reply, banging the window shut before holding my breath and opening it again, just a crack.

Her bladder may be leaky but there's nothing wrong with her ears. 'I've closed it,' I call as I count to the beat of my racing heart.

I love my job. Manager now, you know. Take care of the money, the ledgers and staff. Lock up at night. Deal with disposals.

The odour used to get me down, but now I know better. It's only a smell. Smells can be dealt with.

'Put out your hands,' she'd say, only the once.

I never said no, just closed my eyes and counted.

The water's hot, as piping as I can bear without scalding, and I scrub like she said; back, chest, arms, legs; back, chest, legs and arms, leaving my hands until last. When I'm done I catch her voice from downstairs.

'I've had another accident and I'm wet! I need changing. Can't you hear me calling?'

I don't reply, but scrunch my eyes and hear the words:

'Come down right now or you'll have me to answer to...'

'You're a very wicked boy. I'm counting to ten...'

'Two, four, six...'

'Right, that's it. The kettles going on...'

'Hold out your hands...'

'There now, all done. Good as new. What do we say? Cleanliness is...'

'Shall we throw them out? The odd ones?' Flora asked one day when it was quiet in the shop.

So we tipped up the basket behind the till just before closing. And there it was, the other one, dark brown leather, a real man's glove.

'Just the ticket for your sore hands,' she said, patting my shoulder.

She'd never mentioned them before. I thought she hadn't noticed.

So naked as the day I was born, I'm out of the shower, belting down the stairs and counting odd numbers, ready to swab Mother's piss. But at the door I stop and stare. The room is empty, the wing backed chair has gone, and the breeze through the open window softly rattles the new Venetian blind.

Obese, the doctor said, and dirty - maggots in the folds of her skin - better looked after by professionals.

Stepping to the mirror above the hearth, I study my reflection, impressed with what I see.

Only a proper gent would be made shop manager. And Flora really had to go. She was silly to make such a fuss.

Still, one odour is like another, so nobody notices. And after all, smells can easily be dealt with.

THE PRICE OF SILENCE

Cecilia isn't listening; she's gazing politely, her green eyes on my old grey, but I know her mind is elsewhere. She wants to leave, but she's biding her time. Could she repeat my words if I asked her? Maybe; my Cecilia is clever, very clever. You wouldn't believe it from her serene exquisite beauty, but Cecilia is a dentist.

'Oh, Cecilia. You're far too beautiful to be peering into mouths all day,' I said to her when we met again, entirely by chance on the high street.

Her look in reply was almost inscrutable, but she blinked in a strange way; defensive it was, as though warding off something unpleasant.

'But you always were the brightest girl,' I continued. 'And look at you now, all grown up...'

'I must have had a good teacher,' she replied. She smiled and shook my hand, her nod courteous but final. 'Nice to see you again, Sister Murphy. Goodbye.'

I wrap a curl of her auburn hair around my finger.

It's what I always do when it's time for her to leave. I can't help myself. The spring of silk soothes my rough skin; I bottle the pleasure in case she doesn't come again. Perhaps one day I won't let go and she'll scream and beg me to be kind.

But I wouldn't do that to my Cecilia. She knows I wouldn't.

'Do you enjoy coming here, Cecilia? Do you like being my special friend?' I ask instead.

'You know I do,' she replies.

She brought the children the first time she visited me. Two flame-haired girls and a baby boy, all tucked in neatly with solemn faces. I had the measure of the girls before too long; I hadn't completely lost my touch.

'Will you climb up the stool and fetch the sweetie tin?' I asked the smaller of the two. She didn't even bother looking to her mother for approval, but scooted to the kitchen.

The elder girl looked tense, so I held out my hand.

'You can sit next to me and tell me all about yourself,' I said with a smile. 'You're a pretty girl, the spit of your mommy at your age. I bet you're clever too, and say your prayers. Now don't look so serious, I've all sorts of tales about your mommy if you'll give me a smile...'

'I have to go, Mary.'

Too soon, too soon. It's always too soon.

Cecilia glances at her gold watch, then looks

me in the eye. 'I have to go now, Mary. It's getting late.'

'Five more minutes,' I reply. 'You have five minutes, surely, for old Mary? And I have something for little Maria. Let me see now. Where did I put it?'

And Cecilia waits at the kitchen table, her face blank, her hands neatly folded in her lap.

'Do you believe in pure evil?' I asked, long ago.

'Why, Sister Mary. What a question. Why would you ask such a thing? She's only a child. And look at her face. Such placid beauty is a gift from God. And besides it was just a terrible accident. You said so yourself.'

A Monday, it was, when I visited the surgery. Waited for her last patient to leave, then knocked on the door and walked straight in. Her face was a picture, the panic palpable for moments as the freckled young dental nurse looked on with a puzzled frown.

A smart girl, Cecilia, she composed her face swiftly. 'Oh, hello again Mary,' she said after a beat. 'You managed to find me, then.'

Patches of pink stained her cheeks as she stared at the computer screen. Then she turned, her smile brisk.

'Oh, I see you've registered as a new patient, Mary. Wonderful. So, what can I do for you today? Do you have a particular problem, or is it just a routine check-up? I see you've turned seventy-five, Mary. We'll have to make sure we take special care of you, won't we now.'

'For Maria,' I say, handing over a tiny jewelled statue of Our Lady, one I'd bought in Rome.

Cecilia's face is pallid. 'You can't. It's too lovely,' she replies.

'Of course I can. I want to. Just look at the face. She looks like you. And here are some sweets for little Fiona. She's a rascal that one, has no fear. Maybe more like you than she looks.'

I take another curl and laugh, but Cecilia doesn't smile.

'Maria will love it. Thank you, Mary. Now I really must go.'

'Now, Mary Murphy,' she said on that Monday. 'You've been neglecting your mouth. When did you last see a dentist? I can see I'll have my work cut out here.'

Cecilia's cheeks were rosy, her eyes almost luminous; an echo of the child she was. She smiled with her teeth as she looked at the nurse. 'Mary's a very special old friend of mine. We'll have to do our best to look after her.'

She looked at me softly, her face a blessing. 'There'll be a lot to do at our next appointment, but don't let your nerves get the better of you, Mary. I'll sedate you. It's perfectly safe. Just a little injection and it'll be over before you know it.'

Taking her neat hand in both of mine, I savoured the suppleness of her flesh. 'Come and visit me first,' I said. 'It'll ease my old nerves. I have my own little house these days.'

I looked at the nurse and smiled. 'You'll persuade her, won't you? Just half an hour of her time for this special old friend.'

'Why, Cecilia McConnell. You do look sad. Whatever can be the matter?' I asked, long ago.

'Catherine Maher has been mean.'

'Well, you tell Catherine Maher I'll be having words with her. Rest your head in my lap 'til you're calm.'

'But Catherine Maher says...'

'Don't you worry about her or anybody else. I'll always be here to take care of my little Cecilia. Now I've been making cakes for the priest. Let's share a little one, just you and me. No-one will know.'

Her smile tense, her eyes followed the girls that first visit.

'Yes, have a look at all my books. Do you like reading, young Fiona?' I asked.

The child dragged a chubby finger along the spines. 'Sometimes.' Stopping, she turned. 'What are these ones for Miss Murphy? They all look the same.'

Maria looked on, her green eyes wide. After glancing at her mother, she'd finally selected a packet of sweets from the tin, but she didn't open it.

Holding the baby like a shield, Cecilia was still hovering by the door. I nodded to her.

'You'll get stout legs standing like that, my dear. Come in properly and sit down. We'll have a nice cup of tea.'

Hanged by the Neck

I returned to the younger girl. 'Now, young lady Fiona. You are an inquisitive little thing, aren't you? What were you asking me about?'

'These books, Miss Murphy. They all look the same. They only have numbers on them. What are they for?'

'Oh, so you've found my diaries,' I answered with a smile. 'From as long ago as I can remember. All written in my best handwriting, mind. Maybe one day I'll get them published and be famous. Now wouldn't that be grand? Pick one, any one,' I said. 'And I'll read it to you. It might even be about your Mommy if you're very lucky!'

Cecilia walked from the door, her face pale and calm.

'I think I will have that cup of tea, if you don't mind.' She smiled a best smile. 'That cake does look nice, Mary. Did you bake it yourself?'

'I hated her, Sister Mary,' Cecilia McConnell said long ago.

Her green eyes were luminous, her cheeks rosy pink.

'Of course you didn't. We don't talk of hate here. You're only a little girl and you just feel sad that she's gone. You're much too pretty for hate.'

'I pushed her, Sister Mary. She didn't fall. I hated Catherine Maher so I pushed her. I'm glad that she's dead.'

'Now no more of that silliness. I won't hear another word. I was standing there myself and she fell with the wind. Now rest your head in my lap 'til you're calm.'

'Goodbye, Mary.'

Cecilia kisses my cheek and tears sting my eyes.

'Come on now, Mary. Cheer up. I'll see you next week. I like to keep you happy, don't I?'

I sigh, release the curl and let her go.

TIME FOR SLEEP

Grandpa? Tell me a story, I hear you call. I can't sleep. Tell me a story about the olden days.

I come back and smile; you usually say *tell me a story about a murder*. But tonight you don't - it's late, well past your bed time, and a story of death would frighten you and disturb your sleep. And it would. Really would.

◆ ◆ ◆

'She's crying again. She's always bloody crying, Mother. How can I concentrate on anything with that racket? I just wish she'd stop.'

'Now you know what I have to say about it.'

Gran pulls her sour face which I don't often see. It's like the one she uses when she's sucking a humbug, but that's a happy face - she likes her two ounce ration of mints. Today she's cross with Mam, but I don't understand why.

'At least put her down,' she says. 'You can't go carrying round a screaming bairn when you've got eight hungry mouths to feed. You'll not hear her in the top room.'

'I'll have her Mam,' I say, stepping into the kitchen. 'She stops sometimes for me. Give her here and I'll show you.'

'You're a good lad, Derek. Mind her head, son.'

❖ ❖ ❖

Tell me about your house at the top of the hill, you say, and about your brother and sisters and where you all slept.

Retreating in time, I close my eyes and inhale. Yes, there it is, the familiar dank aroma of clothes drying by an open fire.

There were eight of us, I say, *two boys and six girls. I was the first lad, number four over all. There wasn't enough room in our house, so the older girls went to live with Gran next door...*

What was she like, your grandma? you ask.

And I say: *she was a lovely big lady with a ready smile, a proud bosom and a cloud of white hair.*

What's a bosom? you ask and I laugh.

❖ ❖ ❖

'What's that lump on her head?' John asks.

He's only four and he wants to know. We all want to know.

'She's special, I expect,' I reply. 'And don't mess with her hat. Mam'll go mad.'

I take the bonnet from his grubby fingers and gently pull it back on. The little mite lets me without crying.

'Mam's always mad these days. She never laughs any more. Just leaves me with Barbara and Mags and they're girls,' John says.

'Maybe Grandad'll take you to the match if you're good.'

His face brightens. 'But you're going, aren't you?'

I glance at the clock on the mantle. 'I'll see...' I reply. Then I go back to her perfect face as she sleeps sound on my lap.

◆ ◆ ◆

Tell me about your grandad and bacon, you ask. And though your eyes are wilting, I know it's a funny story you want to take with you to sleep.

There was a ginnel next to our house at the top of the hill, I reply, *and when Grandad was too frail to go to the football match, he'd wait at the top for the first man to come home with the score, and there he would stay until pitch, hoping that the last man home would tell a different tale.*

Did they always lose, Grandpa?

It seemed that way to Grandad but he hated it more when United won...

And that's why he wouldn't eat bacon, you laugh.

Aye, I reply, remembering the smell and the taste of the salty lard. *He said nothing red and white would ever pass his lips.*

Caroline England

❖ ❖ ❖

His body bundled against mine, John's asleep. His nose is blocked from his snotty cold and he's snoring, but nothing drowns out the noise of her cry. It's loud and piercing tonight and I want to go to her. But I know Mam would get mad.

Mam's been mad all day. Shouting and crying and banging the pots. Told us to get out from under her feet, even though there's thick snow on the hills. But when we got to the door, she pulled us all back inside. With a chalky smile, she said she was sorry and that she didn't really mean it, but could we all take turns with the bairn. So I took the baby, but she cried.

❖ ❖ ❖

Night, night I say softly to your closed freckled face.

You smile and breathe out a long sigh, the start of night's oblivion. Stiffly rising from the bed, I turn off the lamp and wish you happy dreams and peaceful sleep.

I pause for a moment to adjust my eyes to the gloom, then head towards the shaft of light breathing in from the landing, and find my cheeks are wet.

It's silent now, but I can still hear the shrill cries which splintered that black night. Wearing my flannel pyjamas, I padded to the landing. As I crept down the stairs, the bawl became louder. Taking care with the creaky step, I crouched in a shivering ball and peered into the kitchen.

Cradling the baby in her arms, my mother was pacing. In a mess of mucus and tears, her face had collapsed, and hair fell wildly from her tight bun.

I almost went to her, but as I leaned a little closer, I saw my grandma was there too. Looking tired but calm, she was sitting by the hearth, her arms folded and fat. Empty glasses were on the table; so they'd had half a beer. Squinting, I wondered what on earth they were toasting, but my surprise was interrupted by the loud scrape of Gran's chair.

She held out her arms. 'Give her to me,' she said above the wailing. Then again, 'Give her to me, Lily,' but more softly this time.

Her face wretched, Mam handed over the baby.

'There, there,' Gran said. And though the baby was still shrieking and flailing pink limbs, her expression was kind. She held her aloft. 'It's not fair, is it, little love? Time for sleep.'

Putting a hand behind her head, Gran drew my baby sister towards her huge chest. And there she stayed until the silence finally came, and the only sobbing I could hear was my own.

A GOOD CLEAN

It wasn't until Ursula was in hospital with a bladder prolapse that she started thinking about it seriously, or so she told us. The thought had apparently popped into her head from time to time, usually when she was waiting for Roger to climax, which was never soon enough, but like a delicious dream, the thought was lost by the inevitable wiping up Roger insisted upon. He was just too fastidious for his own good, was Roger.

'But that's what you get when you marry a heart surgeon,' she always sighed.

I saw Ursula most days, so I'd heard it all before, but the goldfish look on Irene's face did make me smile.

No drifting off in a wet patch for Ursula, not even a towel as a temporary measure. No; Roger insisted on a complete bed change. Not just the bottom sheet either, but the whole lot, floral pillow cases included, which meant a lot of ironing, I can tell you.

'It wasn't as though it was on his side of the bed, the inevitable dribble, but there you go, that's Roger,' Ursula added. 'He'll be wearing surgical gloves next.'

She laughed. It 'hurt her stitches', she said. But that didn't stop her girlish giggle, nothing did.

'Dirty old farts,' Ursula often snorted. 'Men, they're all dirty old farts, they only want one thing and most of them like it down and dirty.'

Except Roger, I expect.

But she didn't say it maliciously, Ursula was never mean. She wasn't like that; 'a generous soul', as my Frank put it, 'easy to please, always was'. A tad overweight, I thought, but still very attractive, we all agreed that. Yes, Ursula was the beauty of our little group, the Wednesday readers. We all had our strong points, and being easy on the eye was hers.

Good job she was so devoted to her Roger and his hygiene, the rest of us said, otherwise we'd all be looking over our shoulders.

So there we were in the hospital. Me, Irene and Joyce, visiting Ursula. Ward 18C on the old East Wing overlooking Junction 23. Right at the end she was, a long walk but very convenient for the toilets, as Irene pointed out.

Ursula chuckled; she didn't 'have need of a loo right this minute,' she said with a wink, wheeling her catheter bag from under the bed.

'Who'd have thought we pass so much,' Joyce said, ever the practical one, and we all nodded, though Irene looked a little pale.

Joyce had helped herself to the last grape when Ursula came out with it, just like that. She'd thought about it from time to time, when Roger was performing - or not - as the case may be.

Irene's chin was still hanging, so I popped in a soft centre. Poor Ursula couldn't eat them, on account of her diabetes. Irene had fetched them, the box of chocolates. That was Irene for you. Lovely woman, wouldn't hurt a fly, but two bob short, if you know what I mean. Thinking wasn't her strong point. Joyce had brought flowers, though they did look a bit past their best, and I presented cake. Taking great care with the ingredients, I'd baked sugar-free carrot for Ursula's dessert. And, of course, I brought a book - the next book.

That's what we did, first Wednesday of the month. Talked about murders. Not real murders, I should add. Fictional ones, from the reads we took turns to select. A crime novel a month, though I invariably fitted in a second without making a fuss. An avid reader I am, you see. Others not quite so. Like Irene. She struggled. Dyslexia, I thought, but Ursula just smiled when I said it.

'Plain Jane super brain, you are, and an angel to boot,' she'd say as I grappled with the Dyson, scrubbed the lav or polished brass, 'We can't all be as clever as you, can we?'

Then she'd giggle. 'But we've all got our talents,' she'd say, reclining on the couch and hitching up her huge bosom in that way of hers.

We'd had to beg or borrow chairs from around the

Hanged by the Neck

ward. 'No sitting on the beds!' the Sister thundered. Poor Irene was quaking in her boots as she'd been the prime offender, albeit perched on the very end like a little wren.

'Have you all washed your hands?' the Sister added, looking at Joyce.

I have to confess I knew what she meant. Joyce was one of those people who didn't look quite clean. I knew she was, of course, but I always rubbed the cutlery with one of my handy wipes when I was at hers, just in case.

'No sex appeal, poor love,' Ursula often commented about her, or rather mouthed it, as she did if she was being a tad less than charitable.

What that had to do with the price of Palmolive, I've no idea.

So there we all were, in ward 18C. She'd 'been thinking', Ursula said. 'The op's been a success and everything's back where it should be...'

We had to lean forward on account of her whispering. She jerked her head like a turkey a few times and I thought she was choking before I realised we were supposed to look behind us at a curious looking man with acne and a stethoscope. He was speaking a bit too loudly to the woman across the ward who'd I'd taken for dead when I borrowed her chair.

Ursula cleared her throat to get our attention again. She was 'as good as new', she said, and 'that nice young consultant', who we'd all gawped at by then, had 'added an extra stitch or two,' if we took her meaning.

Irene clearly didn't. She opened her mouth, the question hovering about her chapped lips, but for once she thought twice and closed it again.

Now she was 'a new woman,' Ursula continued, there was 'no stopping her'.

Ursula couldn't join us for our next book club meeting. *Just Desserts*, the novel was called, an Inspector Harry Henry mystery, and a good read too, though I'd worked out the murderer from the start. Like all good killers, this one had prepared his revenge well in advance and covered his tracks with skill.

Ursula never got round to reading it. Well, she wouldn't, would she; she was dead by then. Unexpected complications with her diabetes combined with a dose of MRSA.

'Must have been you sitting on the bed,' Joyce said to Irene on the Wednesday, which I thought was tall coming from her and her dirty hands.

'More like just desserts,' I was tempted to crow, but it didn't do to brag.

We toasted absent friends and fell silent for a while, each with our own fond memories. I'd miss my daily chores with Ursula watching from the settee, I was sure, but then what, after all, was a halo? It was only one more thing to keep clean.

ABOUT THE AUTHOR

Caroline England was born in Yorkshire and studied Law at the University of Manchester. She was a divorce and professional indemnity lawyer before leaving the law to bring up her three daughters and turning her hand to writing. Caroline is the author of three novels, The Wife's Secret, also called Beneath the Skin, the top-ten ebook bestseller My Husband's Lies and Betray Her. Watching Horsepats Feed the Roses was her first short story collection, Hanged by the Neck is her second. She lives in Manchester with her family.

To find out more about Caroline, visit her website
http://www.carolineenglandauthor.co.uk

Or follow her on social media:

Twitter: @CazEngland
Facebook: http://www.facebook.com/CazEngland1
Instagram: http://www.instagram.com/cazengland1

ALSO BY CAROLINE ENGLAND

The Wife's Secret (also known as Beneath the Skin)
Published 2017 by Avon

Three women. Three secrets.

Antonia is beautiful and happily married. Her life is perfect. So why does she hurt herself when nobody's watching?

Sophie is witty, smart and married to the best-looking man in town. She likes a drink, but who doesn't?

Olivia is pretending to be a happy wife and mother. But her secret could tear her family apart.

Their lies start small, they always do. But if they don't watch out, the consequences will be deadly.

My Husband's Lies
Published 2018 by Avon

Do you really know your friends?

On the afternoon of Nick and Lisa's wedding, their close friend is found poised on a hotel window ledge, ready to jump.

As the shock hits their friendship group, they soon realise that none of them are being as honest with themselves – or with each other – as they think.

And there are secrets lurking that could destroy everything.

Tense, disturbing and clever, My Husband's Lies is a breath-taking read, perfect for fans of Lucy Clarke and Erin Kelly.

Betray Her
Published 2019 by Piatkus

She's your best friend. But can you trust her?

Best friends forever.

That's the pact you made.

You'd do anything for her.

And you have.

She's always had it all.

If you could take it for yourself... would you?

Printed in Poland
by Amazon Fulfillment
Poland Sp. z o.o., Wrocław